Allergic Like

Written by Michelle Meyer-Devlin
Illustrated by Heather Hug

AuthorHouse™
1663 Liberty Drive
Bloomington, IN 47403
www.authorhouse.com
Phone: 1-800-839-8640

© 2010 Michelle Meyer-Devlin. All rights reserved.

No part of this book may be reproduced, stored in a retrieval system,
or transmitted by any means without the written permission of the author.

First published by AuthorHouse   12/6/2010

ISBN: 978-1-4520-9463-2 (sc)

Library of Congress Control Number: 2010917433

Printed in the United States of America

Certain stock imagery © Thinkstock.

This book is printed on acid-free paper.

To Julia,
For whom I am so proud

When Annie was little
even younger than three,
her parents discovered a food allergy.

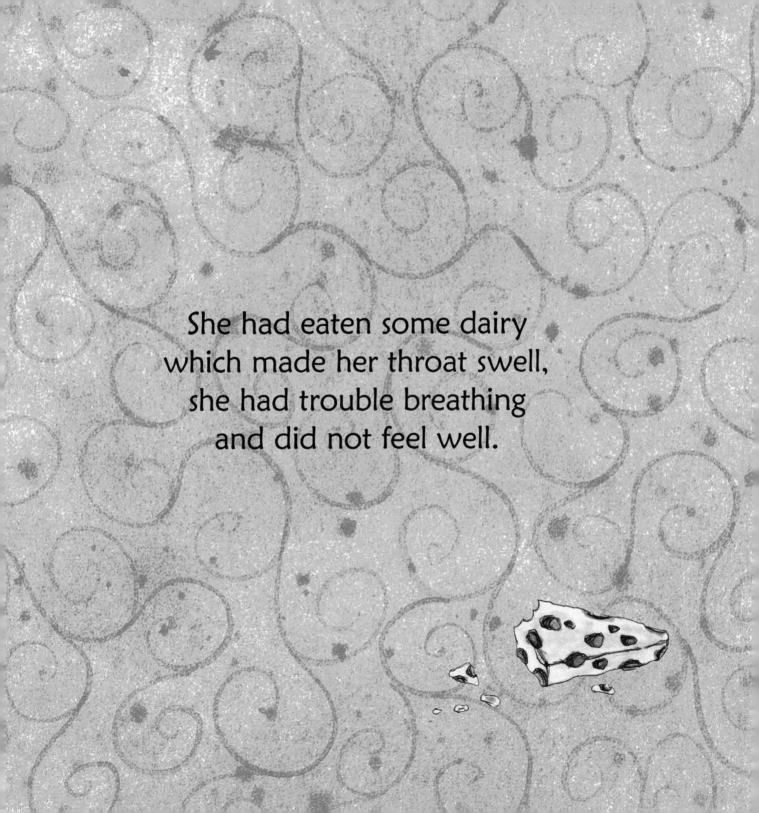

She had eaten some dairy
which made her throat swell,
she had trouble breathing
and did not feel well.

No pizza, no ice cream and even no cake,
no eggs and no butter, "was this a mistake?"

Mom says I'm special
one day I will see,
it's ok to be allergic like me.

She did not feel special
she felt very sad,
that at birthday parties
no treats could be had.

"Don't worry" said Mom,
"you will get to have cake.
It will be *special* cake, that I will
gladly bake."

And Halloween came
Annie did trick-or-treat,
but most of the candy
she could not eat.

Her Dad let her trade
which still made it fun,
two candy pieces
for each chocolate one!

My Dad says I'm special
one day I will see,
It's ok to be allergic like me.

The holidays came.
Christmas was here.
"Do you think Santa knows
I'm allergic this year?"

Santa did come and brought lots of treats.
Candy canes, lollipops and things she could eat.

Annie got older and went off to school.
"I am sure being allergic is very un-cool."
"Not true!" said her mom.
*One day I will see; it's ok to be allergic
like me.*

She met with the principal
and with the school nurse,
"You can bring medication
in a cool purse."

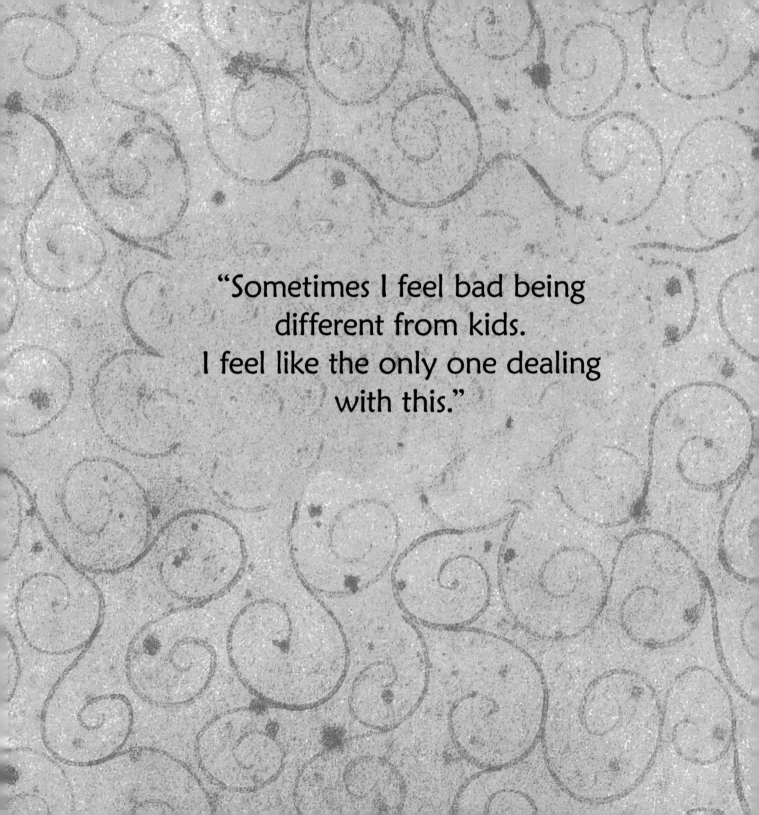

"Sometimes I feel bad being
different from kids.
I feel like the only one dealing
with this."

"Not true," said the nurse.
Annie then came to know,
lots of kids have allergies
and they do not show.

MILK and DAIRY and SOY and PEANUT
SHELLFISH and WHEAT and GLUTEN and TREE NUT
DOGS and CATS and allergic to TREES

Lots of kids have these allergies!

Annie has lots of friends;
they all do know,
she brings her owns foods
wherever she goes.

Her friends are so nice
they go out of their way,
to make her feel special whenever they play.

"My parents were right"
Annie says with much glee….

"IT'S OK TO BE ALLERGIC LIKE ME!!!"

10 25 '03

Michelle Meyer-Devlin and her husband Frank Devlin, found out their daughter, Julia, was allergic to dairy at the age of 9 months. As she grew older, it was difficult to explain why she could not always share in events and parties the same as other children. Michelle wrote this book to help parents educate their children on some trials they may face when managing a food allergy. This photo is Julia on her 7th birthday with her "dairy free" cake.